MY NAME IS BEAR!

For Rob and the diners: Katybob, Laura and Lucy – N.K.

EGMONT

We bring stories to life

First published in Great Britain 2019
by Egmont UK Limited,
The Yellow Building, 1 Nicholas Road, London W11 4AN
www.egmont.co.uk

Text and illustrations copyright © Nicola Killen 2019

Nicola Killen has asserted her moral rights.

ISBN 978 1 4052 9245 0

A CIP catalogue record for this title is available from the British Library

MY NAME IS BEAR!

Nicola Killen

Once there was a bear called Bear,
who had just moved to a new home.

Bear loved his name **so much**
he couldn't wait to introduce
himself to **everyone**.

Soon Bear met his first neighbours.
"Hello! My name is **Bear**."

"Hello!
Pleased to meet you.
My name is **Bird**,"
said Bird.

"And my name is **Fish!**"
said Fish.

"Fish? Bird? They're the **silliest** names I've **ever** heard," said Bear.

And with that,
he went on his way.

How rude!

On the other side
of the wood,
Bear spotted some
napping neighbours.

"Hello!"
he shouted.
"My name
is Bear!"

"Oh . . . hello. Pleased to meet you. Our names are Snail and Tortoise," yawned Snail and Tortoise together.

"What **odd** names! I bet you wish you were called Bear," said Bear.

And on he went.

This bear has such bad manners!

As Bear met more and more neighbours, his comments got **ruder** and **ruder**.

"My name is Elephant," said Elephant.

"What? Smelly pants?" laughed Bear.

"My name is Lemur."

"Really? Poor you!"
Bear snorted.

"My name is Meerkat."

"Is that even a name?"
spluttered Bear.

He's unbelievable!

The more names Bear heard, the prouder he felt.
Bear was the **best name of all!**

The next neighbour Bear met
looked a little familiar . . .

"Hello!
My name is Bear."

"Hello!
My name is Bear,"
said the other bear.

He's not going
to like this...

"What?" cried Bear. "You can't be called Bear. That's my name!"

Bear got redder and **redder**...

And crosser and **crosser**... Until –

"MY NAME

"IS BEAR!"

he shouted.

What a tantrum!

"We could always share our name?"
suggested the other bear helpfully.

Bear didn't like that idea.
"You could be **Mr B?**"
he suggested instead.

The other bear definitely
didn't like that idea.

"I'm a girl!"

She didn't want to
be called Beary or
Bear Two either . . .

. . . so after a lot of talking
and **even more** thinking, Bear **finally**
agreed to share his lovely name, and they
celebrated with a **big bear hug!**

Hooray!

Bear took his new friend to meet
all the neighbours.

"Hello, everyone. This is Bear!"

"**Hello!**" said Lemur,
Bird, Elephant, Fish,
Snail, Tortoise, Meerkat
and Worm, too.

They hoped **this** bear
had better manners.

Hello!

As Bear got to know his neighbours,
he realised they all had lovely names
which really suited them.

He owed them a **big** apology.
"**I'm so sorry!**" he said.

And as Bear's neighbours got to know him properly,
they realised that Bear wasn't quite as rude
as he first seemed.

What a relief! —

A few days later a new
neighbour arrived.

He looked quite like Bear,
and the other bear too . . .

"Hello" said the
new neighbour.
"My name is . . .

Uh-oh!

...Crinkleton
Wiff-Waff
Maximilian
Shufflebottom!"

Everyone looked
nervously at Bear . . .

Was he going to say something rude?

"Crinkleton Wiff-Waff
Maximilian Shufflebottom!" said Bear.
"What a **wonderful** name!"

Phew!
Bear had learned
some manners at last.
Well done, Bear!

I love
a happy
ending!